TUNES
FOR BEARS
TO DANCE TO

TUNES
FOR BEARS
TO DANCE TO

Robert Cormier

Delacorte
Press

Published by
Delacorte Press
Bantam Doubleday Dell Publishing Group, Inc.
666 Fifth Avenue
New York, New York 10103

Copyright © 1992 by Robert Cormier

The trademark Delacorte Press® is registered in the U.S. Patent and Trademark Office.

LIBRARY OF CONGRESS CATALOGING IN PUBLICATION DATA

Cormier, Robert.
    Tunes for bears to dance to / Robert Cormier.
      p.   cm.
    Summary: Eleven-year-old Henry escapes his family's problems by watching the wood carving of Mr. Levine, an elderly Holocaust survivor, but when Henry is manipulated into betraying his friend he comes to know true evil.
    ISBN 0-385-30818-3
    [1.   Holocaust   survivors—Fiction.   2.   Prejudices—Fiction.
3. Family problems—Fiction.   4. Artists—Fiction.]   I. Title.
    PZ7.C81634Tu   1992
    [Fic]—dc20   92-2734
                                                           CIP
                                                          AC;r92

Manufactured in the United States of America

October 1992

10 9 8 7 6 5 4 3 2 1

BVG

To Fabio Coen

With my great thanks

*Human language is like a cracked kettle
on which we beat out tunes for bears to dance to,
when all the time we are longing
to move the stars to pity.*

—GUSTAVE FLAUBERT

Deliver us from evil.

—OUR FATHER

The old man came out of the crazy house every morning shortly before eight o'clock and walked down the graveled path to the gate, carrying a small leather bag that swung like a pendulum from his right hand. His moustache was a wedge of frost on his upper lip.

The boy, whose name was Henry, watched him from the third-floor piazza that overlooked the street. He was curious about where the old man went every day and would have followed him except for the cast on his knee. The cast would be removed in a week or so and he tried to be patient in the meantime, watching the comings and goings of the neighborhood. The most interesting thing he saw was the old man. Why did he live in the crazy house and why did they let him out every day if he was crazy?

—◆—

"You shouldn't call it a crazy house," his mother said. "It's an institution for the insane."

That was worse than calling it a crazy house, Henry thought. Anyway, the old man did not look either crazy or insane. The boy saw him only for a few moments as he came and went, but he looked normal enough. In the late afternoon when the old man returned from wherever he went, his steps were slower, spiderwebs had appeared around his eyes, and his shoulders drooped although his cheeks were still smooth, like stones worn away by years of rain.

Henry hobbled up to the gate of the crazy house once in a while and looked at the people strolling the grounds. They looked normal, too, like the people he saw every day in the neighborhood.

The boy himself did not feel normal. He had never learned to use the crutches properly in the five weeks he had worn the cast. He tripped over them all the time. He was not coordinated or athletic, like his brother, Eddie, and walked awkwardly with the crutches, which is why he seldom left the piazza.

Eddie would have mastered the crutches in no time at all. He would have swung down the street, calling out to everyone, and everyone would have smiled back. Henry tried not to think about Eddie but that was impossible, of course. Although Eddie had been dead almost a year—eleven months and three days, to be exact—he was still a presence in the lives of Henry and his mother and father. Sometimes Henry felt guilty because he could go, oh, three or four hours without thinking of Eddie, but his mother and father seemed to be thinking of him every minute of the day, walking wearily and sorrowfully through the hours, seldom talking except when necessary. His father, in fact, was swallowed up in his sorrow. Sometimes, Henry could not stand the silence in the tenement and went out on the piazza. Once he thought of jumping over the banister and plunging to the pavement below but knew that would only bring more sorrow to his parents.

He was impatient for the cast to be removed so that he could return to his job as the bender for Mr. Hairston at the Corner Market. Mr. Hairston had a back problem and found it hard to bend over. Henry did the bending for him. Picked up whatever fell on the floor. Reached for merchandise on the lower shelves to fill the customers' orders. He also had other duties. Helped unload the boxes and crates that arrived from the wholesalers. Stocked the shelves. Put up potatoes, fifteen pounds to a peck, in the cellar, then carried them upstairs to the produce section. Mr. Hairston was proud of his produce. Fresh lettuce and carrots and spinach and such extras as parsnips and mushrooms, all of them in neat display at the rear of the store.

Henry worked at the store every day after school and on Saturday mornings. Until, that is, he broke his kneecap, tripping, then falling down the bottom steps of the three-decker just as school ended in

June. A hairline fracture, the doctor said, nothing serious, but serious enough for a cast that enclosed his calf and knee. Mr. Hairston said he would keep his job open until his knee was healed.

"How will you bend over?" Henry had asked.

"I won't stock the lower shelves until you come back," Mr. Hairston said.

"Who'll sweep the floors and put up the potatoes?"

Mr. Hairston scowled and did not answer. He scowled most of the time, his expression as sour as the pickles in the wooden barrel near the cash register.

Henry didn't want to say what he said next. But had to say it. "Jackie Antonelli would be a good bender for you. He lives on my street. He's in my class at school."

He waited in dread for Mr. Hairston's answer. He didn't want Jackie Antonelli to take his job away from him. He had promised Jackie that he would ask, although he did not care particularly for Jackie, who liked to fight. His family was poor, Jackie said, and could use the money. But everybody in that section of Wickburg was poor and could use the money.

"Jackie would work hard," Henry said, hating himself for saying that, not knowing whether Jackie *would* work hard.

"Jackie Antonelli's a greaseball," Mr. Hairston said. "I don't want a greaseball working for me."

Henry was relieved but immediately filled with

guilt because of that sense of relief. He was also angry at Mr. Hairston for calling Jackie a greaseball. Yet he was not entirely surprised at Mr. Hairston's remark about Italians.

Mr. Hairston's favorite pastime was standing at the window near the big brass cash register, watching people passing by on the street, and making comments about them.

"Look at him, Selsky. A kike. Charges too high for his goods. Always running a sale but jacking up the prices before the sale, then coming down a little. . . ."

Or:

"There goes Mrs. O'Brien. An Irisher. Nine kids. Spends most of her time in bed. But not sleeping." Then, a strange grunt, like a pig squealing, which, Henry learned, was the way Mr. Hairston laughed.

Or:

"Look at her, Mrs. Karminski. . . ."

The boy saw Mrs. Karminski huffing and puffing as a small dog that looked like a windup toy pulled her along the sidewalk.

"Sloppy," Mr. Hairston said. "Too much rouge on. Pampers that dog. Pays good money for dog food. Leaves her house and lets her slip show. Dumb. A Polack."

"I think she's lonesome," Henry said, making an exception, because he usually didn't talk back to Mr. Hairston. "Her husband died last month." Just before Henry broke his kneecap. "I saw her crying

yesterday when she was walking her dog. Her
cheeks all wet . . ."

"A disgrace," Mr. Hairston said, "making a
spectacle of herself, crying in public. She should cry
at home. And him, her husband. Bad breath. When
he came in here, his breath almost knocked me
down."

They watched Mrs. Karminski being tugged
around the corner by the small dog.

"What a world," Mr. Hairston said.

"Sad," Henry said, thinking of Mrs. Karminski
and her husband with bad breath who was dead.

"Not sad, terrible," Mr. Hairston said. "The war
is over, sure, but now the Bomb. Could kill us all, in
a flash. Just as well maybe. Too many people in the
world. Too many stupid people."

He was interrupted by the arrival of a customer,
Mrs. Lumpke, who was never without her red hat,
like an upside-down flowerpot, on her head. Henry
was glad for her arrival. Most of the time Henry kept
busy in the store and avoided Mr. Hairston's company and his remarks. Yet Henry was grateful to Mr.
Hairston for having given him this job.

Henry had been new in the neighborhood when
he was hired. His father had not worked since Eddie
died. He had not gambled, either, and seldom left
the tenement. His mother had found a job in the
Miss Wickburg Diner downtown, but the pay was
small and the tips did not amount to much. Henry
had roamed the neighborhood, homesick for the

people and streets of Frenchtown in Monument. His parents had not been able to stand Frenchtown since Eddie's death and they had moved here to Wickburg, a bigger city twenty miles away. They were lucky to find the third-floor tenement next to the crazy house, because war veterans were given first priority by landlords, and the new housing projects were strictly for veterans. Henry's father had not gone to war. Something wrong with his ear, a punctured eardrum, the doctors said. Which made him unable to stand the terrible noises of war. So they moved into the tenement next to the crazy house, which Jackie Antonelli thought was disgraceful although Jackie himself lived only three houses away.

Henry shrugged away Jackie's remark, just as he endured Mr. Hairston's comments. His big disappointment in the new neighborhood was that his parents showed no signs of recovering from Eddie's death. They had not left Eddie behind in Frenchtown, after all. He lurked everywhere in the tenement even though there were no pictures of him on display, and all his trophies remained in boxes on the closet shelf in Henry's bedroom. Eddie had won the trophies for his athletic exploits. He could run faster and leap higher than anyone else. He swung a bat with such authority that he thrilled the crowd even when he struck out. He was terrible in school, not like Henry who always made the honor roll and never got into trouble. Eddie wasn't a good student, hated to do homework, and often skipped. All this was forgiven, however, because everyone knew he was destined for greatness on the ball field. He would someday wear a Red Sox uniform and hit home-run balls over the big wall in left field at Fenway Park. He died instead, sprawled in the gutter of First Street in Frenchtown, his neck broken like a chicken bone snapped apart to make a wish. The car that had struck him sped away and was never seen again.

The morning after the cast was removed from his leg, Henry followed the old man when he left the crazy house.

He was pleased that his knee didn't bother him as he walked along behind the old man. He had winced at the sight of his leg, pale and a bit shriveled, when the cast came off at the doctor's office. But he walked normally enough as he followed the old man in his erratic progress through the streets.

If the old man was not crazy, he was certainly strange. His lips moved as if he was carrying on a conversation with an invisible companion. Once in a while he stopped walking and stood silently, staring at nothing in particular, caught in a sudden trance. Then he tipped his black cap, a kind of beret but with a visor, and resumed walking. He tipped his cap several times although there was never anyone to tip his hat to.

For an old man he walked fast. Henry had to be alert because he took unexpected shortcuts through alleys and backyards. Henry's leg began to weaken, as if it was hollow inside, and he limped a bit but was able to keep the old man in sight most of the time.

Finally they arrived at a section of town Henry had never visited before. Old ruined buildings leaned against each other as if for support. Down the street young guys hung out in front of a barroom matching coins they tossed in the air. The old man stopped at a store that appeared to be vacant. The windows were painted black and there was no sign above the big front window where a sign should be. The old man put down his black bag and leaned against the window frame, as if catching his breath. Then he tipped his cap again, picked up the black bag, and knocked at the door. He disappeared inside as the door opened.

Henry rubbed his chin and kicked at a tin can on the sidewalk. Curiosity itched him, like a mosquito bite. He saw the guys in front of the barroom staring at him, suspending their game with the coins. Noting a narrow alley next to the vacant store, Henry cautiously made his way toward it, then dashed into the alley. He emerged at the far end into a bleak landscape of sagging fire escapes, overflowing rubbish barrels, and abandoned furniture, like debris from a shipwreck. A gray rat squirted between two piles of old wooden crates.

◆

A newly painted red door drew his attention, no doubt the back door to the store the old man had entered. Stealthily, feeling like an actor in a Saturday-afternoon movie serial, Henry advanced toward the door and tried the handle. Gently but firmly. The door did not open.

After glancing around to see if he was being observed or if the barroom guys had followed him, Henry leaned over and looked in the keyhole. A foolish action, of course, sensible in a movie but ridiculous in real life. As expected, he saw nothing.

Suddenly, the door swung open and Henry almost fell on his behind, his jaw dropping in surprise as a huge man, a giant of a man, appeared in the doorway.

"What're you doing here?" the giant bellowed, his voice like the wind of a hurricane.

Henry could not speak, helpless before the giant.

"What're you snooping around for?" the giant demanded, stepping forward. Which made Henry scurry backward, causing him to trip this time and fall to his knees. He winced as pain shot through his healed kneecap and he wondered, *Have I broken it again?*

The giant towered above him, suffocatingly, his bare arms bulging with muscles, his legs like tree trunks.

The pain in Henry's knee went away, leaving

◆

the hollowness. He was dismayed to find his cheeks wet with tears.

"Hey, I'm not going to hurt you," the giant said, his voice suddenly gentle. "Did you hurt yourself when you fell down?"

Henry shook his head as he got to his feet, wiping at the tears on his face.

"You want to see what's going on inside?" the giant asked. "Is that it?"

Henry tried to shake his head but couldn't move a muscle. He wanted nothing to do with this giant, gentle voice or not. What if he was crazy like the old man?

"I didn't mean to scare you, boy," the giant said, a sad smile revealing big jagged teeth. "But we have trouble here with some of the neighborhood wise guys. . . ."

Scrambling to his feet, Henry looked up into the giant's eyes for a moment—soft brown eyes that were full of regret—then tore himself away, stumbling, the giant's voice trailing behind him as he ran for the alley:

"Wait . . . don't go. . . ."

But Henry kept going, grateful that his bad leg was strong and sturdy again as he ran through the alley.

Later, making his way home, he was sorry that he had not gone into the store. He wondered if he would ever find out what the old man was doing inside the place or what his black bag contained.

Mr. Hairston merely grunted when Henry reported to the store without his crutches, ready for work, that afternoon. Henry had scrubbed his face and combed his hair. His leg still felt strong despite his long run home that morning.

"Potatoes to put up," Mr. Hairston called over the shoulder of a customer, and Henry made his way down to the cellar, where a bin of potatoes awaited him. He always tried to hurry the job because the cellar was dark and damp and he often heard rats scurrying across the floor. One day, a gray rat squirmed out of a bag of potatoes and Henry had leapt with fright, his heart exploding in his chest. He was afraid of a lot of things—the closet door that never stayed closed in his bedroom, spooky movies about vampires—but most of all, the rats.

When he came back upstairs, Mr. Hairston was saying good-bye to a customer Henry recognized as Mrs. Pierce, who lived on the first floor of his three-decker. Smiling and nodding, Mr. Hairston led her to the door and closed it softly after her.

"Disgusting, the wart on her chin, hairs growing out of it," he said, returning to the register, a sneer replacing the smile. Actually, his smile was not really a smile—just as his laughing was not really laughing—but a mere rearrangement of his lips, his usual sneer turned inside out.

Henry was amazed at how politely Mr. Hairston treated his customers, smiling and bowing and eager to please when they were in the store, and how insulting he was when they were gone.

"The customer's always right," he proclaimed one day, as if he could read Henry's mind. "But only in the store. When buying. Otherwise, they're only people. Stupid, most of them. Don't even know a bargain when they see one. So, why give them a bargain?" He handed Henry a Baby Ruth bar, which astounded the boy because Mr. Hairston had never before given him a treat. "Eat," he said. Then: "It was nice with the customers during the war, though. Rationing. People came running if they heard I got butter in. Or cigarettes."

Henry listened, his cheeks bulging with the candy while Mr. Hairston looked off, as if he were talking to himself, his voice almost dreamy. "I'd make them line up. Make them wait, acting like the

◆

stuff hadn't arrived yet but was expected any minute. All the time the order was here and they waited in line. I was like a dictator, the way they treated me. I *was* a dictator. Because I had control over them." Then looking down as if discovering Henry's presence after having forgotten him there, he said, "Go to work. I don't pay you to hang around doing nothing."

Just before closing time, while Henry was sweeping the floor, Mr. Hairston's daughter came into the store. She appeared at the back door, having descended from the tenement above, where Mr. Hairston lived with his wife, whom Henry had never seen, and the girl, whose name was Doris. Doris was a whisper of a girl, slender, with long black curls that reached her shoulders, a bow in her hair. It looked like always the same bow but the colors were different, red and yellow and blue, bright and vivid colors in contrast with her pale white face, the dark eyes deep in their sockets, like the windows of a haunted house.

She usually came and went like a ghost, appearing suddenly and then fading away, a door closing softly behind her or the rustle of her clothing faint in the air. Sometimes he didn't see her at all but sensed her presence somewhere in the store. She was a year ahead of him in school and when they met in the corridor she lowered her eyes and looked away. She always carried library books in her arms. In the store he sometimes felt those haunted eyes upon him, turned and almost saw her, then heard the back door closing softly. They had never spoken a word to each other.

Whenever Mr. Hairston saw her in the store, he ordered her to leave. "Upstairs," he commanded, his hand pointed to the ceiling.

That afternoon the girl spoke to Henry for the first time, a brief word: "Hello." So brief and whispered that at first he doubted his ears. She didn't smile at him but her expression changed, or rather an expression of some kind filled the usual blankness of her face. He could not read that expression. As she turned away before he could return her greeting—if it *had* been a greeting—he noticed a bruise on her cheek, purple and ugly.

"What happened to your cheek?" he asked, whispering for some reason.

"Upstairs."

Mr. Hairston's voice was like thunder in the quiet store and Henry leapt with surprise as he turned to confront the store owner, whose face was dark with anger.

Henry began to sweep furiously and heard the girl's footsteps fading, the door opening and closing.

"She fell down," Mr. Hairston said while Henry swept the same spot over and over. "Clumsy girl, always hurting herself."

A late customer entered the store and Mr. Hairston turned away, cursing beneath his breath. He hated last-minute customers.

◆

That night Henry added Doris to his prayers as he knelt beside his bed. He said his prayers every night as the nuns at St. Jude's Parochial School back in Frenchtown had taught all the students to do. He prayed first for his mother, small and delicate, who had worked the night shift during the war, coming home at dawn, white with fatigue, trying to sleep in the noises of the day. Now she was a waitress, standing on her feet all day and carrying heavy trays. He then prayed for his father, deep in his silence. He prayed that his father would begin to gamble again, even if gambling was the reason there was never enough money in the house. His father, too, worked in the wartime shops but gambled away his earnings most of the time, a hard-luck gambler willing to bet on a ball game or a horse race or on the cards in his hands but seldom winning. Now his father didn't gamble anymore and Henry prayed for him to come out of his grief even if it meant gambling again and losing as usual.

He also prayed for Eddie, in case he was not in heaven. But where else could he be? Certainly not hell. Eddie had never done anything to deserve hell. Purgatory? Maybe. The nuns had often spoken of that place where souls waited to be admitted into heaven. Souls got into heaven from purgatory if enough prayers were offered on their behalf. So, Henry prayed for Eddie's soul, taking no chances that he might not yet have reached heaven, hoping to nudge him closer each night.

"And deliver us from evil," he murmured. "Amen."

Before making the sign of the cross, ending his prayer, he thought of Doris who was clumsy and fell down a lot and hurt herself. He prayed to keep her safe from harm. Then he added a prayer for the old man, asking Jesus to watch over him. Anyone who lived in a crazy house certainly deserved a prayer.

The next day, Henry followed the old man again, more curious about his actions now —the way he tipped his hat, his changes of expression, his sudden trances—than his destination.

Turning a corner, he was startled to find that the old man was nowhere to be seen, as if he had disappeared from the face of the earth.

Suddenly he stepped out of the shadows of a doorway, his black bag clutched to his chest for protection, his hands trembling as they held the bag, his eyes wide with fright.

Blushing furiously, Henry said, "Don't be afraid." He had never seen such fright in someone's eyes.

The old man backed away, cringing now, as if expecting a blow.

"I'm not going to hurt you," Henry said, gen-tling his voice, wondering if the old man understood what he was saying. "I'm only eleven years old. . . ."

Perhaps his words or the regret in his voice took some of the fear away, because the old man halted his backward steps and relaxed his grip on the bag. Big tears filled his eyes now and spilled onto his cheeks, dampening the white moustache.

Tears blurring his own eyes, shocked that he had frightened such an old man, Henry heard him-self saying, "I've been watching you every day and wondered where you went, that's all. My leg was broken and my brother is dead. . . ." He was amazed that he was confessing such things to this old man, a stranger.

Wiping his cheek, the old man said, "Dead?" Or a word in a heavy accent that sounded like *dead*. Then a sound Henry had never heard from a man or woman before, an anguished cry from deep within: "Aaaaayyyy . . ." Like the sound someone makes when the pain is too much to bear, the load too heavy to carry, the heat too hot, the cold too cold.

Touching the old man's shoulder, grateful that he did not pull away, Henry said, "It's all right. My leg is better now and my brother is in heaven." He did not mention the possibility of purgatory.

The old man nodded his head and fell silent, although his cry still echoed in Henry's ears. They

◆

stood silently together, ignoring the people who looked at them curiously as they passed by.

Raising his hand and beckoning, the bag no longer a shield for protection, the old man said, "Come." Henry fell into step beside him, offering to carry the old man's bag. The bag was not heavy at all but rattled with whatever was inside. Henry pretended not to notice when the old man tipped his cap occasionally, although he did not pause or go into one of his trances.

When they came in sight of the store, he saw the giant pacing the sidewalk, all bone and muscle. It was a wonder the pavement did not tremble beneath his feet. The giant shouted with relief when he spotted the old man. He spoke a few words to him in a language Henry did not understand, then explained, looking down at Henry, "I was worried about him because he was late. You can usually set your clock by him." Scrutinizing Henry from his lofty height: "So, you came back . . . good."

The giant led them into the store.

It was not a place of deep dark secrets after all but a big room where a dozen people busied themselves at benches, heads bent in concentration, fingers flying everywhere. At first Henry thought the store had been converted into some kind of factory. Machines whirred at some of the benches, sending showers of dust into the air. Other people worked quietly with their hands. Green-shaded lights threw pools of brilliance on the benches.

As the old man made his way to a sheet-covered bench, the giant said, "This place was once a pool hall, but now it's an arts-and-crafts center. People come here who can't afford lessons. Or don't have enough money for supplies. Some are artists who need a place to work. Some just need a place to go. The city of Wickburg pays for all this. . . ."

In one corner a tall, thin man squinted at a half-finished painting of birch trees against a bright blue sky. A few feet away a round woman with blue hair massaged a big lump of clay. When Henry narrowed his glance, he saw the head of a child emerging from the clay.

Turning away, amazed at the swarm of activity, Henry saw the old man pull the sheet off the bench, revealing a miniature village of houses and barns, populated by tiny wooden figures, not more than an inch or two in height.

"Mr. Levine is a wood carver," the giant said. "He's re-creating the village of his youth there on the bench."

"Is that his name, Mr. Levine?"

"Yes, Jacob Levine."

"My name is Henry. Henry Cassavant."

"And I'm George Graham," the giant said, a smile revealing his big teeth.

George Graham? Henry thought that a giant like this man should have an imposing name, like the heroes in books, Thor or Ivan.

Mr. Levine looked back at Henry, then gestured

at the wooden village, smiling. But there was some-thing sad in the smile, Henry thought. The old man opened his bag and set small tools out on the bench.

"See those buildings and the tiny figures?" George Graham asked. "He told me they look ex-actly like the people he knew in that village long ago. He's a real artist, Henry."

Henry stood beside Mr. Levine as he went to work, putting the finishing touches to the figure of a child, barely an inch high, carving gently with fin-gers that never faltered, holding the small cutting tool securely but tenderly.

On the bench before him an entire village was laid out. Cottages, barns, stores. Animals in the fields, horses and cows, mules and chickens and dogs. All of them in their natural colors. And the figures, like real people. Women with bandannas peeking out of windows or hanging clothes on a line, men standing in the streets of the village. Carts and wagons.

The old man worked steadily, taking a break only to put down the figure and tip his hat to no one in particular, and then resuming his task. Once in a while he glanced at Henry and smiled, the smile be-coming familiar to Henry now, a smile tinged with not-quite-sadness, not-quite-happiness.

George Graham strolled through the center, stopping to talk to the people, nodding, touching a shoulder here and there, listening intently as they talked. Most times he knelt on the floor beside the

artists, and thus was at eye level with them. Every
once in a while laughter filled the air as the people
called to each other or visited one another's benches
to see the work in progress. A boy only a few years
older than Henry was turning a wine jug into a
lamp, while beside him a young woman swollen
with pregnancy stitched pieces of cloth into a quilt.

George Graham returned to the old man's bench
and knelt down beside Henry.

"Are you an artist too?" Henry asked.

"No, I run places like this for the city. We have
branches all over Wickburg. But this one is my favorite."

"How long does it take him to make those figures?" Henry asked.

"Five or six hours each. He is the most patient
man I've ever met."

Mr. Levine turned and gestured to Henry to
come closer. He picked up a small block of wood
with one hand, a razor blade with the other. He began to whittle away at the block of wood.

"That's balsa wood," the giant explained. "Soft,
easy to work with, not like the oak he uses for the
village."

Henry watched the curved head of a duck
emerging, then the beak. The swift passages of the
blade caught the light. The finished specimen was
rough, but unmistakably a duck. The old man applied a brown dye to the wood, stroking quickly
with a small brush. He turned, paused, and handed

it to Henry, a wide smile on his face, no hint of sadness at all in the smile now.

"Thank you," Henry said.

The old man nodded and said something in the strange language to George Graham.

"He says the pleasure was his, that your presence here gives him pleasure," the giant relayed to Henry.

"What language was that?" Henry asked.

"Yiddish, an old language from his country in Europe."

"Are you Yiddish too?"

George Graham smiled gently. "Yiddish is a language, Henry. Spoken by Jews. But I'm not a Jew. I'm good with languages, that's all. I served as a translator for the army during the war."

Holding the carved duck delicately in his hand, Henry watched the old man as he resumed work on the figure of the child, with a cutting tool so small that it was almost invisible in his hands. The curved cheek of the girl formed itself under the tool's strokes.

Finally Henry knew it was time to leave. There were chores to perform at home, a list in his pocket his mother had handed him before she left for work.

He touched Mr. Levine's arm.

"I have to go now," he said. "Thank you for the duck."

The old man nodded in acknowledgment, held out his hand, and their fingers entwined themselves.

At the door, the giant said, "Will you come again? Mr. Levine is alone in the world. Has no family. . . . His wife dead, and his children. I think you remind him of his son. He looks at you fondly. . . ."

Fondly . . . a tender word on the tongue of this huge bulk of a man.

"I'll come back," Henry promised.

Henry and his mother took the bus to Monument every Sunday to visit Eddie's grave. The ride was bumpy, the smell of exhaust heavy and suffocating despite the open windows. When the bus arrived in Monument, they walked a mile or so to St. Jude's Cemetery on the edge of Frenchtown. They never went back to their old neighborhood. "Too many memories," his mother said. Henry knew the unspoken word—*sad*. Too many sad memories. Eddie's death had obliterated all the good times they had known in Frenchtown.

At Eddie's grave his mother exchanged last week's wilted flowers for new ones. The flowers made Henry sad. He had never heard Eddie say that he liked flowers. What boy did? But what else do you bring to a cemetery?

Henry and his mother knelt down, lips moving soundlessly as they prayed. Henry did not look at his mother, because he knew her face would be stark with grief. *Why do we come here?* he wondered. There was no comfort in the cemetery. Eddie's grave was maintained by St. Jude's parish but was forlorn and lonely, without a stone to mark it.

"Why don't we have a stone for Eddie?" Henry asked, although he suspected the reason.

"We will someday, Henry," she said. "When things get better. . . ."

"When Pa starts working again?"

"Yes," she said, looking away.

"But what if he starts gambling again?"

"Maybe he'll start winning," she said.

"Why is he a gambler, Ma?" he asked. Henry had always been puzzled about his father's all-night card games, why he preferred the company of men in smoky back rooms to being home with his family.

"Know what he really is, Henry?" Not waiting for an answer, she went on: "He's a dreamer, your father. He dreams about what a windfall will do for us, if he makes a killing."

The gambling words—*windfall* and *killing*— sounded alien on her lips and also funny in a sad way, her voice wistful as she spoke them.

"But he doesn't gamble anymore," Henry said, still trying to solve the puzzle of his father. "And he's so sad, Ma."

"More than sad, Henry," his mother said.

◆

"When sadness becomes too much to bear, it becomes a sickness. As if your father's standing in the shadows."

"Because Eddie died?"

"We all have our own way of handling the bad things that happen, Henry," his mother said, staring down at the grave. "The doctor said it will take time. . . ."

He was amazed to find out that sadness could be treated like a disease and that his father had actually gone to a doctor. He was disappointed that his mother had kept the doctor a secret from him. But what of his own secrets? He had never told her or anyone how much he missed Eddie, or his homesickness for Frenchtown and his old pals, Leo Cartier and Nicky LaFontaine, or his bad dreams in which an atomic bomb exploded and a huge mushroom cloud obliterated the world.

"Poor Henry," his mother said, tousling his hair, her touch tender. Then, with determination: "Look, if you think we should have a stone for Eddie's grave, then we'll have one." She bent down and picked up the water jar, holding it as if it was a grenade she was about to toss. "One way or another."

"Maybe we can save for it," Henry offered. "A little bit from your pay and a little bit from mine."

"Maybe," his mother said.

The impossible suddenly seemed possible, and Henry did a little dance of excitement there in front of Eddie's grave. Then paused. "What kind of stone, Ma?"

They looked at the surrounding gravestones, slabs of gray, blocks of granite, forbidding in their loneliness. Even a nearby stone in the shape of an angel was grim and remote.

"Something special," she said, her eyes bright and lively. "Something that would please Eddie to have it here. What do you think he would like, Henry?"

Henry thought of Eddie and his love of baseball, his air of confidence as he stood at the plate, coiled and ready to hit, swinging the bat impatiently as he waited for the pitcher to throw the ball, and then a magnificent swing, the crack of the bat meeting the ball, and the ball soaring like the arc of a rainbow toward the farthest point of the field. And the shouts and hoorays from the stands.

"A bat and a ball," Henry said, the words popping out of his mouth.

His mother regarded him with astonishment, openmouthed, then turned to look down at Eddie's grave. Henry also looked down, picturing a baseball bat and ball arranged on the grave like the symbols of the 1939 world's fair, the bat standing erect and the ball at its base.

They looked at each other and began to laugh at the thought of such a monument. The first time he had seen his mother laugh since Eddie died. Her laughter bubbled merrily in the air and Henry joined in. They were suddenly helpless with laughter, as if they had been released from a long imprisonment. Seized with such merriment, they clutched each other, giving themselves to the sudden joy of the moment.

"Can you imagine," his mother said, pausing to catch her breath, "what Father Lemieux would say if he saw a bat and ball on Eddie's grave?"

Later, as they made their way out of the cemetery, the stone path crunching beneath their feet, he touched her arm and pointed to a remote spot where the land sloped upward. The spot contained the children's section, where the stones, from this distance, resembled tiny baby's teeth. They had ventured there one day but had never returned to that forlorn spot. Stones in the forms of lambs and teddy bears and doves stood above the small graves. Small toys had been left near the stones—a red plastic truck, a blue ball, a small wooden horse.

"If Father Lemieux allows lambs and teddy bears, maybe he won't mind a bat and ball," Henry said.

"It doesn't matter what he thinks," his mother said. "If we want a ball and bat for Eddie, that's what we'll have."

Henry wanted to throw his arms around her but withheld himself, afraid she might thrust him away as she sometimes did when she was tired and irritable or probably lonesome for Eddie.

In the hush of late afternoon, between surges of customers—they always come in bunches, like bananas, Mr. Hairston often complained—Henry approached the grocer where he stood at the window, commenting sourly as usual on the people passing by.

"Do you know anything about monuments, Mr. Hairston?" Henry asked.

"What kind of monuments?" the grocer asked absently, still looking out the window.

"Monuments for a cemetery," Henry said.

Looking with narrowed eyes at Henry, the grocer said, "What's all this about monuments? Or is it an excuse to stop working for a minute?"

Warmth flooding his cheeks, Henry picked up the broom and began to sweep the floor, although he had already swept it.

◆

"Okay, okay," Mr. Hairston said. "Put down that broom. Sweeping a clean floor is a waste of energy better spent elsewhere. And I remember now— your brother is dead and the monument is for him, am I right?" But no apology in his tone or manner.

Nodding, Henry said, "My mother and me, we're planning one for his grave. What I'd really like is to save up and buy one for him myself." Impossible, of course, but nice to think about, to even say aloud.

The grocer turned back to the window, as if no longer interested.

"Where do you go to buy a monument?" Henry persisted.

"You go to a place that sells them," Mr. Hairston said, laughing that piglike laugh that was without mirth or amusement.

"Where do you find such a place?" Henry asked, refusing to be discouraged.

Mr. Hairston sighed, his shoulders lifting and falling in resignation, and turned to the boy again. "You buy a monument like anything else. You shop around. There's a place near Oak Lawn Cemetery that sells them. A man named Barstow owns it. Makes a good living at it, I guess. Must be a big markup—all you have is a stone with names and dates."

"Is his place far from here? Can I take a bus there?"

Mr. Hairston squinted at him, his eyes bright

suddenly with interest. "You're really serious about this?"

Henry nodded. "My brother deserves a monument. I think he's the only one in the cemetery without one."

"What kind of monument are you thinking of?"

Henry wondered: *Should I tell him? Will he laugh?* He hated to say anything to spoil Mr. Hairston's sudden interest. But why not go the whole way?

"Eddie was a great ballplayer. I was thinking of a ball and bat."

Mr. Hairston did not frown or scoff, did not make his strange squeal of a laugh, but continued to look at Henry with his deep dark eyes.

"I know this Barstow. I'll talk to him."

Henry felt his jaw drop open in disbelief, like in the funny pages. He blinked. Had he heard Mr. Hairston say what he thought he'd said? He dared not ask. Instead he murmured, "Thank you," having to clear his throat to utter the words, and began to sweep the same spot.

The next time Henry went to the craft center the old man was working on another tiny figure, wielding the delicate cutting tool painstakingly, his entire body bent in concentration.

A tall stool had been placed beside the old man and he motioned for Henry to sit down, nodding and smiling, evidently pleased that Henry had returned. Henry again was in awe of the village and the carved figures, so lifelike that he expected them to suddenly walk and talk.

George Graham came and knelt beside them and the old man spoke to the giant in that odd Yiddish language.

The giant listened intently, then said to Henry, "He wants to know if you would like to learn wood-carving."

Henry had always been without talent. He was

not good at sports like Eddie. He had taken piano lessons for three months from Sister Angela at St. Jude's and failed miserably. In school his worst subject was art. He saw visions in his mind of what he wanted to draw but could not transfer those visions, or even a hint of them, to paper.

"I don't think I'd be very good at it," he said.

"Try it," George Graham urged.

Mr. Levine held up a small knife and handed it to him. Henry took it, holding it gingerly. Mr. Levine picked up an identical knife, then a small block of balsa wood, similar in size to the duck he had carved for Henry.

For the next few minutes he guided Henry in the first tentative steps of carving, placing Henry's hands in correct positions, guiding his movements, his touch light as a snowflake on Henry's skin.

Flakes of wood fell away. Henry became aware for the first time of the smells surrounding the bench, the clean smell of wood shavings and the sharp odors of shellac and dyes, a confusion of smells that made his nostrils itch. A shape began to form in the wood. Did he have talent, after all?

Then a slip of the knife, a brief slicing downward, and Henry saw blood spurt from his finger before he felt the pain. Moving quickly, Mr. Levine drew a white cloth from somewhere and wrapped it around Henry's finger. The pain was not severe, although blood seeped through the cloth, bright and vividly red.

The old man moaned and sagged against Henry. The giant was instantly by their side.

"He can't stand the sight of blood anymore," George Graham said. "Or to see anyone in pain."

Forgetting the pulse of pain in his finger, Henry looked inquiringly at the old man. His face was whiter than his moustache, his lips as if stained from eating blueberries. The giant murmured gently to him, as if soothing a frightened child.

Later, Mr. Levine apologized through the giant. "He is sorry that he let you cut yourself and for collapsing like that."

As the old man continued working, his fingers trembling a bit, the giant said, "There is so much evil in the world, Henry. That's why Mr. Levine faints at the sight of blood. That's why he sits here day after day rebuilding his village, and the people in it, trying to bring them back. . . ."

"Did something bad happen to his village?"

"The Nazis happened. They turned the village into a concentration camp. Burned down some of the buildings, made others into barracks to hold prisoners. Then they built chambers where people were exterminated. The villagers were either killed or sent away or put to work. Mr. Levine and his family were separated. His wife and two daughters were taken away to a camp called Auschwitz. He never saw them again. He and his son, who was twelve, were put to work in the village, building the chambers. His son died that first winter, without medicine to help him."

"How did Mr. Levine escape?" Henry asked, watching the old man slice a curl of wood away from the figure in his hand.

"He didn't escape. He survived. He was beaten and starved. But he's a tough old man and not as old as he looks. The camp made him old, the deaths of his family. When the war ended, the Allies set the prisoners free, Mr. Levine among them. The world finally recognized what had been going on in all those camps. How millions had died . . ."

Henry had learned from newspaper headlines and newsreels at the movies about Hitler's hatred of Jews, how he wanted to rid an entire race of people from the planet. He remembered pictures of bodies piled like logs of charred wood that were discovered at the end of the war. But those bodies had been far removed from his life. Now he shivered as he looked at Mr. Levine, and the war suddenly came alive for him, all these years later.

"When the soldiers found Mr. Levine in the camp, he was only skin and bones. He was covered with sores. He could not hold food in his stomach."

"Why is he living in the crazy house?" Henry asked, lowering his voice, hoping Mr. Levine could not hear him ask such a question.

"Not only his body suffered," George Graham said, also speaking low. "His mind and his nerves were shattered. He still has terrible nightmares. The

━━━━━━━━━━━━━━━━━━━━━━━◆━━━━━━━━━━━━━━━━━━━━━━━

hospital here is helping him to adjust, to start a new life."

As they watched, the old man tipped his cap, to no one in particular. "Know why he does that?" the giant asked. "Another remnant of Nazi cruelty. The guards in the camps played cruel games. Made the prisoners do exercises, like push-ups, for hours at a time. Outdoors, in the wind and the rain. In heat or cold. Sometimes all night long. They also made the prisoners tip their hats at the sight of a guard. Made them repeat the gesture for hours on end. If they did not tip their hats or whatever they wore on their heads, they were knocked down, kicked, and beaten. Tipping the hat became reflex action. So now he tips his hat and doesn't even know he does it."

Mr. Levine worked on, lost in his miniature world.

"This is his real cure, better medicine than the hospital," George Graham said. "He's bringing his village, and the people who lived there, to life again. His wife and children. His friends and neighbors. Even the village bully everybody hated, the fat one with the red jacket. During the time Mr. Levine works here, he's back in the village again. Sometimes, at the end of the day, he sits quietly, gazing at the village, touching the figures. I think at those moments he is at home again with those he loved, walking the streets, courting the girl who would become his wife. Once when I called to him that it was time to leave, he didn't hear me. I sat in the shadows watching him. He sat there for two hours, and I knew he was home again, in another time and place. . . ."

Even now, as the giant talked, Mr. Levine put down his tool and the carved figure and, sighing, looked down at the village. Henry and the giant sat there, also silent and still, watching him. The three of them sat like that for a long time until someone called that it was time to close the center for the day.

Jackie Antonelli stood at the corner of their street, near the Welcome Bar, hands in his pockets. Since Mr. Hairston's refusal to hire him Jackie sent glowering looks Henry's way whenever they met, as if he blamed Henry for not getting the job.

"Still living next door to the crazy house?" Jackie called.

Henry looked up to see the smirk on his face. It was a stupid question and Henry did not bother to answer, stepping around Jackie.

"Know who belongs in the crazy house?" Jackie called, hunching his shoulders the way tough guys did in the movies.

"Who?" Henry asked, although he was not interested.

"Your father, that's who!" Jackie said, voice flat

♦

and deadly. Then in singsong fashion: "Your father doesn't work. Your father doesn't leave the house. Your father should be in the crazy house."

Henry flew at him, reaching for Jackie's throat, engulfed by a rage he had never known, a rage that brought blood to his eyes. Jackie fell back, a muffled scream coming from his mouth, and Henry fell with him, the jolt loosening his grip on the boy's throat. Jackie's arms flailed at the air, his legs kicked, his entire body thrashed and twisted, while Henry pummeled him.

"Quit that, stop that," came a rough voice from somewhere. Strong hands pulled the boys apart, sending Henry reeling away.

Jackie scrambled to his feet, massaging his throat. "What are you—a madman?" he yelled hoarsely.

The man who had separated them was a veteran who still wore his khaki uniform, faded and patched up now. He hung around the Welcome Bar day and night. He had stormed the beaches of France on D day and people said he had never slept a wink since then, awake twenty-four hours a day.

His eyes red and bleary, breathing heavily as if he had run a long distance, the veteran muttered, "What's the matter with you kids?" His voice filled with disgust. "Don't we have enough fighting in the world?"

"He attacked me," Jackie whined, his voice still

rough-edged. "I didn't do anything. We were stand-ing there talking and he started to choke me."

"My father is not crazy," Henry said, pronounc-ing each word distinctly, needing to impress the truth on Jackie Antonelli and the veteran and people who had begun to gather. "He's sad but not crazy. . . ."

"Get out of here, the two of you," the veteran said. "Vamoose."

At home Henry's father sat at the kitchen table shuffling cards with one hand, the cards slipping and sliding in and out of the deck.

"It's hot out," Henry said, raising his voice a bit, speaking as if his father was deaf. Sometimes he seemed to be deaf and did not respond when some-one spoke to him.

Slowly gathering the cards into a neat pile, his father looked up at him.

"I'm sorry, Henry," he said.

Sorry for what? The heat? This tenement? His long silences? His father spoke so seldom that Henry gave weight to everything he said.

"Don't be sorry, Pa."

"You're a good boy," his father said. He seemed about to say more, wetting his lips with his tongue, then fell into silence again and resumed shuffling the cards.

Henry waited a few moments, glad to have heard his father's voice, then went outside to the piazza. His mother was late, which meant she was working overtime again. He looked down at the deserted suppertime street. He thought of Frenchtown and how Leo Cartier used to call his name after supper on nights like this: "Henry, are you coming out?" *I will not let myself be lonesome,* he vowed silently.

His mother arrived, bringing anger into the tenement. Not only had the tips been bad today but some customers had stiffed her, which meant they had left without paying the check. Two young guys in sharp suits. The manager, Mr. Owens, had taken it out of her pay. "I like you, Aggie," he had said. "But I've got to set an example. Otherwise someone will play an angle on me." All this Henry heard her report to his father. His father did not reply.

She banged pots and pans and dishes around in the kitchen. Then silence fell. Henry slipped down the front stairs. He could not at this moment bear to be in that sad tenement.

"See the old man out there, tipping his hat to nobody," Mr. Hairston said at the window. "Looks like an idiot."

The boy put down the feather duster and went to stand beside the store owner.

"That's Mr. Levine," he said.

Surprise on his face, Mr. Hairston asked, "And who's Mr. Levine?" Brusquely. "I know he's a Jew by his name, but who is he?" He scowled fiercely, as if angry at Henry for knowing a Jew.

"He lives in the crazy house, but he's not crazy," Henry answered. "He was in a concentration camp during the war. His village was destroyed by the Nazis. His family was killed, his wife and children, all his relatives."

Mr. Hairston made no reply. Kept staring out the window. "Look, he's tipping his hat again. I think he *does* belong in the crazy house."

"That's reflex action," he said, using George Graham's words. "The guards made him tip his hat so much in the camp, and beat him up if he didn't, that now he does it all the time." Henry felt the explanation was inadequate. "He's a nice old man."

"Watch out for Jews," Mr. Hairston warned. "Even a nice old one."

Did Mr. Hairston hate everyone? Henry wondered.

"He's very talented," Henry said.

"Talented? What kind of talent does an old Jew from the crazy house have?"

"He's rebuilding his village that was taken by the Nazis, carving the houses and barns and shops. Carving small pieces of wood to look like the people he grew up with. The village is beautiful."

"Well, I hope it keeps him out of mischief," Mr. Hairston said. "You never can tell about these people."

Later, when Henry had finished dusting the cans on the shelves and polishing the fruit, Mr. Hairston summoned him to the window. He hoped that the grocer would discuss the monument, whether he had talked to Mr. Barstow yet.

"Tell me more about the old man," he said. "That village he's making."

Heartened by the grocer's interest, Henry repeated all that the giant had told him about the Nazis and what had happened to Mr. Levine's family.

Eagerly he described the old man's painstaking work on the miniature buildings and figures.

"Five or six hours for every figure?" Mr. Hairston asked, obviously impressed. "How many figures? How many buildings in the village?"

"A lot," Henry said, his mind racing to compute the number. "A whole village of people. Young kids and fathers and mothers and *pépères* and *mémères*," using the old French words for grandparents. "The buildings aren't too hard to make, but the little figures take a lot of time. You should see him work at them, Mr. Hairston. He's a great artist. The figures look exactly like the people he knew."

"Interesting," Mr. Hairston said. And said no more, sending Henry away with a fling of his hand and remaining at the window, silent and thoughtful.

Henry was uneasy as he resumed work, as if somehow he had betrayed the old man.

After Henry had helped to unload the merchandise from the delivery truck, he lingered for a moment on the platform, letting the cool air bathe his face.

He turned at a sound from the far end of the platform and saw Doris standing in the shadows of the staircase. She emerged slowly, walking delicately, as if her bones would come apart and clatter to the floor if she moved too quickly.

"Are you all right?" Henry whispered. She was the kind of person that you spoke to in whispers.

She nodded, almost imperceptibly, wincing, as if even the movement of her head was painful.

"Your father says you fall down a lot," Henry said. "Did you fall down again? Is that why it hurts you to walk?"

"It doesn't hurt me to walk," she said, a bit defiantly but only a bit, as if she was trying to convince herself as well as Henry. Then, looking away: "Yes, it does. . . ."

"How did you fall down?"

She looked at him sharply, opened her mouth as if to answer, then clamped her lips shut.

Henry made a sudden leap of knowledge. "You didn't fall down, did you?"

She looked at him with those deep dark eyes and still did not say anything.

"Do you like to read?" she finally said. "My father lets me go to the library whenever I want." A hint of boasting in her voice.

Henry did not answer.

"I'm clumsy," she said, lifting her shoulders and sighing. "I drop things sometimes and he gets mad."

Henry felt a rush of tenderness for this thin pathetic girl. He almost reached out to stroke her cheek.

"Be careful of my father," she warned, speaking low again, glancing toward the back door of the store.

"Will he hurt me too?" Henry asked, stunned at her words.

"There are a lot of ways he can hurt," she said. "He never hits my mother, but hurts her with his tongue, the things he says to her. . . ."

"What does he say?"

"That she's dumb and ugly. And too fat. That she eats too much."

What kind of man was this Mr. Hairston who hit his daughter so hard it hurt her and called his wife dumb and ugly?

Perhaps Doris saw the questions in his eyes, because she said, "My father loves me and he loves my mother. But he wants us to be perfect." The small defiance returning.

"But he's not perfect," Henry said. "In fact, he's . . ."

Doris waited for him to say more but Henry did not know what Mr. Hairston was, and he shrugged his shoulders.

Now Doris was timid again, almost shriveling into herself as she drew away. "I have to go," she told him, her voice low and barely audible. "I shouldn't have said what I said to you. Try to forget I said it. . . ."

She turned away and Henry watched her shuffling slowly, painfully, toward the stairs. The stairs creaked as she climbed them, like the sound of her wounded bones.

A crazy thought, he told himself, but the sound lingered in his ears the rest of the afternoon.

"Stay awhile after I cash up," Mr. Hairston said. "I have something to show you."

Ordinarily, Henry was free to leave the store when the six o'clock whistle blew at the fire station down the street, signaling the end of the business day. When Henry went out the door, Mr. Hairston was always busy at the cash register, counting the money and entering various amounts into a ledger.

"Have a Baby Ruth while you wait," Mr. Hairston said. Baby Ruth was his favorite candy bar, which the grocer had offered him only once before. He knew that eating the candy would spoil his supper but hesitated to rebuff his boss. Chances were that supper might be late anyway, because his mother often worked overtime at the diner.

While Henry chewed listlessly, the caramel sticking to the roof of his mouth, Mr. Hairston continued to enter figures into the ledger. Finally, he closed the ledger and looked at Henry, a strange expression on his face. Strange for Mr. Hairston, that is, because his face was almost pleasant, his features suddenly soft, not sour as usual.

The grocer opened a drawer in the counter and drew out a sheet of paper. He placed it flat on the counter and motioned for Henry to approach and look at it.

The paper showed a black-and-white drawing of a stone monument, the name EDWARD CASSAVANT at the bottom in fancy letters. Above the name were a baseball bat and ball embedded in the stone, the bat upright as Henry had envisioned, and the ball, stitchings visible and scarred a bit like a real ball, at the base of the bat.

Henry's throat tightened. He had no words to describe a thing of such beauty. Taking his eyes reluctantly away from the sketch, he looked up with gratitude at the grocer.

Then looked away, thinking dismally, *How could we afford such a monument?*

"Well, what do you think?" the grocer asked.

Henry detected eagerness in the grocer's voice, something he had never heard before. He was uncomfortable as Mr. Hairston waited for his reaction, his eyes fastened upon him. This was a Mr. Hairston he had never encountered before.

"It's beautiful," Henry said, the word inadequate. "But how much will this cost?"

Mr. Hairston shrugged and opened the ledger, became busy with it again, studying the entries as if he was looking for a mistake he had made. He mumbled something that Henry did not catch.

"I don't think we could afford a monument like this," Henry said reluctantly, placing the sketch on the counter.

Mr. Hairston looked up, coughed and cleared his throat, and said, "Maybe we can work something out. . . ."

Henry had been about to turn away when Mr. Hairston's response struck him like a lightning bolt. *Struck* was exactly the word. There was no thunder and no storm, only *maybe we can work something out.*

Then, regarding Henry with that same soft expression the boy could not identify, Mr. Hairston said, "We'll see."

Magic words, *we'll see.* What his mother and father said when they did not want to say *yes* right away. *We'll see,* meaning not *no.* Not *yes,* either, of course, but in the country of *maybe* and *perhaps,* where everything was possible. *We'll see,* words of hope a breath away from *yes.*

Henry managed to remain still, rooted to the spot, resisting the urge to shout or dance. He was about to ask Mr. Hairston if he could show the sketch to his mother when the grocer said, "All right, off with you." Reverting to his usual gruffness. "My supper's getting cold upstairs. She's a terrible cook, my wife, but the food doesn't taste too bad if it's hot at least. . . ."

On the way home Henry decided not to mention the sketch to his mother, not until *we'll see* became *yes,* so as not to disappoint her if it didn't.

At home he found his mother sitting in the parlor, in her best blue dress, white high heels on her feet and a white straw hat on her head. His father was also dressed up, in his gray Sunday suit, a red tie flowing like blood on his white shirt. This was not Sunday but Thursday, and Henry felt as though the earth had suddenly spun out of orbit.

"Are we going someplace?" he asked, apprehensive, because his mother's lips were set in a grim line, her lipstick harsh against her pale skin.

"Your father is going to the hospital," she said.

To the crazy house? he wanted to ask, remembering Jackie Antonelli's taunts. But instead asked, "Will they make him better there?"

"I hope so," she said. "Please don't be upset, Henry. It's the best thing for him."

"What kind of hospital?" Henry said, lowering his voice, yet knowing his father could hear him because he was sitting at the table only a few feet away. But he had to know.

"Not like next door," she said, sensing his fear. "A regular hospital, but they have a section for people like your father who need special help."

"It will be all right, Henry," his father said. "Listen to your mother."

"What you must remember, Henry, is what I told you," his mother went on. "His sadness is a disease and they have medicine to treat diseases."

"Can't he take the medicine at home?" Henry asked, hating the thought of his father in a special section of a hospital.

"Well, it's more than medicine, more than just pills he needs," his mother said, uncomfortable now, clasping and unclasping her white purse.

"What does he need?" Henry asked, intent on knowing the whole truth, afraid of secrets, yet afraid to know, afraid to even look at his father at this moment.

"Therapy."

An ominous word, with rumblings, mysterious, threatening. "What's therapy?" he asked.

"Something to bring your father out of his sadness," she said. Then, her voice softer: "Don't worry about it, Henry. It's for his own good." *His own good.* These were also ominous words, words his mother spoke when he had to take bitter medicine for a cold or do something unpleasant. *For your own good.*

"Will it cost a lot of money?"

"We'll manage," she said. "I'm going to see if I can work double shifts for a while. . . ."

A horn sounded outside.

"The taxi," his father said.

"Where is this hospital?" Henry asked, almost in a panic. "Can we visit you there?"

His father looked at his mother.

"It's here in Wickburg, on the south side," she said. "We can take a bus to visit, but a taxi's best to take him there."

His father came to Henry and kissed his forehead. His lips were cold. "Be good to your mother," he murmured.

When they were gone, Henry pounded the top of the sofa with his fist. It was better than crying. Then he cried anyway.

❖ ❖ ❖

The next afternoon Mr. Hairston did not acknowledge Henry when he showed up for work. Henry greeted him with his usual "Hello, Mr. Hairston, how are you?" but the grocer merely grunted as he stared out the window.

Henry began his chores without having to be told what to do: sweeping the floors, rearranging the fruit and vegetables that had been disturbed by morning customers, unpacking six boxes of Campbell's soup that had been deposited on the back platform. Between trips with the boxes into the store he kept a lookout for Doris, but the girl did not appear.

Henry tried not to think about his father in the hospital. *Think about the sketch,* he told himself, *and whether Mr. Hairston will show it to you again.* As he carried out his chores, Henry glanced at Mr. Hairston occasionally but the grocer, between customers, kept his vigil at the window, muttering his usual sour comments about the people passing by.

Every afternoon when business dropped off and customers were few, Mr. Hairston disappeared into the meat locker, where he would slice sides of beef into steaks and grind up scraps of meat for hamburg. Henry knew that would be his chance to slide open the drawer in the counter and look at the sketch. The grocer stubbornly remained at the window, however, as the afternoon went on.

Henry slipped into the locker to check on the supply of steaks and hamburg. He was glad to see that only a pound or two of hamburg remained. He hoped that Mrs. Carson would show up. She always bought at least three pounds for her big family. Dusting the shelves near the front door, Henry glanced expectantly at the door when customers entered, but Mrs. Carson did not appear.

Finally, Mr. Hairston touched Henry on the shoulder. "Hamburg," he said, nodding toward the locker. "Call me." Which meant, of course, that Henry should summon the grocer when a customer entered the store, an unnecessary order that Mr. Hairston never neglected to issue.

Henry kept busy with the duster. It was a mystery to him where dust came from day after day. He worked his way to the counter, paused, and looked toward the locker, satisfied that the grocer would not have a clear look at the counter if he came out unexpectedly.

Henry stalled, in sweet agony, wanting to glance at the sketch but filled with guilt at the prospect of acting behind the grocer's back. What if a customer entered and Mr. Hairston emerged from the locker at the same time? He remembered that the drawer also contained the grocer's ledger and other stuff and he would probably have to search the drawer for the sketch. Yet it drew him irresistibly.

A minute passed, two, as Henry watched the clock on the wall. No customers entered. He heard, dimly, the hamburg grinder at work. His fingers touched the handle of the drawer. The grinder lapsed into silence and he looked toward the locker. Glanced out the window. No customers in sight. He pulled the drawer out of the counter, slowly, wincing at the squeak of wood against wood. Looked down. Miraculously, he saw the sketch immediately on top of the ledger. Then moaned. Not a moan exactly but a sound of doom escaping his lips.

The reason for the sound of doom.

A terrible X, crisscrossed lines in heavy black crayon, slashing across the sketch, harsh lines of cancellation that also canceled Henry's hopes for the sketch to somehow become a reality.

Later, as Henry took off his apron and prepared to leave for the day, Mr. Hairston told him that he was being fired at the end of the week.

W hat Mr. Hairston actually said was:
    "Your services will no longer be re-
quired here."
He spoke formally, as if talking to someone
standing above and some distance beyond Henry.

"Today is Wednesday. Your last day of work
will be Saturday."

At first Henry refused to accept the meaning of
the words the grocer spoke. His mind became blank,
like a blackboard suddenly wiped clean. Then their
meaning became clear and his body sagged, as if all
the air had been sucked out.

"Have I done something wrong?" he asked, his
mind scurrying to remember any mistakes he had
made. Had Mr. Hairston seen him peeking at the
sketch? Was that cause enough to fire him?

Mr. Hairston turned away as if Henry had not
spoken.

♦

"Why am I being fired?" Henry persisted, sim-
ply angry, knowing he had done a good job in the
store, had not been lazy, had performed to the best
of his ability.

"You have outlived your usefulness," the grocer
declared, turning to the cash register. "I do not need
you any longer." Then, regarding Henry with eyes
that held no hint of mercy: "You have the rest of the
week to work. Don't shirk your duty on those days."

The words reverberated through his mind as he
sat on the tenement steps the next morning watching his mother going off to work, her steps slower
than usual. He had heard her tossing and turning
alone in her bed last night. He had decided not to
tell her about being fired. Not until it actually happened. She did not need more bad news these days.
Although Henry's pay at the store was small, his
mother always accepted the money with gratitude
on payday. "Every bit of money helps," she said. "I
don't know what I'd do without you, Henry." And
now the job was lost.

His mother turned the corner and gave a last
wave. From this distance she looked pretty enough
to be a movie star. He was glad that she was too far
away for him to see the blue shadows under her
eyes, the strands of gray that had begun to show up
in her black hair.

He lingered on the steps for a while, watching
the neighborhood activity as people went off to
work. Before eight o'clock arrived, he sauntered

down the street, not wanting to see the old man coming out of the crazy house.

He spent the next few hours listlessly wandering the streets, sighing often, kicking at stones on the sidewalk. Killing time. Paused now and then to watch the lobsters in the window of the fish market, walked on the steel rails of the B & M tracks, sat on the bridge over the Quinsig River, dangling his legs as he watched a man painting a boat.

He was tempted to visit his father at the hospital, although his mother had said that visits were forbidden during his first week of therapy. He realized dismally that he did not know the location of the hospital, which made his father seem even more distant from him.

Finally he headed for the craft center, a better place to be than the tenement at home, where a tasteless cheese sandwich awaited him for lunch. Worse than the dry sandwich were the empty rooms.

The clapping of hands and shouts of celebration greeted Henry as he opened the door. Astonished, he thought at first the applause, impossibly, was for him. Stepping inside, he saw the people in the center focused on Mr. Levine, surrounding him at his bench.

George Graham spotted Henry at the door and beckoned him forward. "Big news, Henry," he called. "Mr. Levine has won first prize from the city for creating the best work of art."

The old man inclined his head modestly, his

hand reaching out to touch one of the small figures in the village. With his other hand he tipped his hat, while people regarded him with pride and pleasure.

"His village is going on display at City Hall," the giant said. "Under glass. Decorated with a blue ribbon. A big ceremony. The mayor and city council will be on hand. Reporters, too, and maybe TV coverage . . ."

"Congratulations," Henry said to the old man. Tears appeared in Mr. Levine's eyes, but not the tears of that first day, because his eyes were merry.

"You're a good boy," Mr. Levine said, pronouncing the words slowly but distinctly.

"You see?" the giant said. "He's been rehearsing, wants to speak better to you."

"Invite . . . invite," the old man said, looking appealingly at the giant.

"Oh, he wants to invite you to the ceremony. Saturday afternoon. We're all going. At two o'clock."

"You come?" the old man asked Henry.

Henry nodded, then looked at the village, the tiny figures that he recognized now like old friends.

"This village," the giant said, "will be a reminder to everybody about what happened during the war. But also about survival. And how good can overcome evil. That's what this village symbolizes." Then the giant looked abashed, and actually blushed. "Speech over . . . let's celebrate," he said.

At that moment, as if on cue, the ladies of the center appeared with a big white cake, easily two feet high, topped by a flaming candle.

Mr. Levine came forward, his eyes dancing with delight, and Henry forgot for a few moments about being fired and his father receiving therapy in the hospital.

When he arrived at the store, Mr. Hairston was waiting on Mrs. Lumpke, who wore her flowerpot hat as usual. Today she was stocking up on Campbell's tomato soup. A dozen cans. Henry carried her order out to the sidewalk, where he placed the two heavy bags in a wicker baby carriage. Mrs. Lumpke did not have a baby but used the carriage to do her shopping. "You're the best worker Mr. Hairston ever had," she said, smiling at him. Which only made Henry feel sadder than ever.

In the store Mr. Hairston grunted as Henry said, "Good afternoon." The grocer busied himself with paperwork at the cash register and did not look up.

Henry went to the cellar and began to put up the potatoes. He worked listlessly, taking no pride in the job, filling the bags automatically, weighing them

◆

without interest, adding a few potatoes or taking some away until the scale registered fifteen pounds. He did not even keep his eye out for rats.

The door at the top of the stairs opened, spilling light down on the steps. Henry looked up and saw the figure of Mr. Hairston silhouetted in the doorway.

"You want to keep your job?" The grocer's voice boomed down as if he were shouting in a tunnel.

Henry nodded, staring up into the shadow that was Mr. Hairston's body.

"Say yes or no," the voice commanded.

Henry swallowed, cleared his throat, said, "Yes." Then again: "Yes." Not wanting the grocer to misunderstand.

"Good," Mr. Hairston said. "Work hard this afternoon. Before you leave, I'll tell you how you can keep your job."

Customers streamed in and out of the store that afternoon, the cash register constantly ringing. Mr. Hairston waited on them eagerly, exchanging pleasantries about the weather, making small jokes, laughing now and then. Henry had never seen him so cheerful. He did not make his usual rude remarks after the customers left. Hummed as he worked at his figures.

Finally, at the end of the day, Mr. Hairston closed the front door and lowered the shade that said CLOSED on the outside. Henry waited by the cash register. Mr. Hairston went to the counter and pulled out the drawer. He reached in and withdrew the sketch, held it up for Henry to see. The terrible *X* had been removed; only smudges remained as a reminder of its existence.

"Do you see the *X* mark has been removed?"

Henry nodded, perplexed.

"You peeked at it, right? I knew you would be sneaky and peek at it. That's why I put the *X* on it. You only appreciate something when you think you have lost it. I wanted you to appreciate it."

But I did appreciate it, Henry thought, wondering why Mr. Hairston would do a thing like that.

Mr. Hairston placed the sketch on the counter, looking down at Henry with those merciless eyes.

"You don't want to lose your job, do you?" he asked.

Henry shook his head, swallowing hard as if something was stuck in his throat.

"You also want a monument—this beautiful monument here"—indicating the sketch—"for your brother's grave."

Henry nodded, not trusting himself to speak.

"Fine," the grocer said. "You can keep your job."

The late afternoon sun blazed through the window, exposing dust motes in the air, dust that would later settle on the shelves.

"The monument for your brother? I spoke to my friend who drew the sketch. He will make that mon-

♦

ument. With the best stone from a quarry in Vermont. It will be my gift to you."

Astounded, Henry thought, *But for what?*

The question echoed in Henry's mind before he asked it. "But for what?"

"A simple thing."

What simple thing?

"What do I have to do?"

"What you have to do is easy," Mr. Hairston said, leaning back against the wall, eyes half closed, as if envisioning what Henry had to do. "It requires no skill at all, just a bit of effort. Maybe a bit of cunning. I know that Canucks are not famous for cunning, a bit stupid in fact, not cunning like the kikes. But everybody has a bit of it. . . ."

Henry waited, blinking away the insults, not sure what *cunning* meant.

"What I want you to do is this," Mr. Hairston said, looking directly at Henry. "I want you to go to that craft center one day next week. On any day you choose. In the afternoon."

"But I work for you in the afternoon."

"That day you won't. But I'll pay you just the same."

"Okay," Henry said, puzzled, frowning, a bit uneasy.

"When the center closes for the day—you said it closes at six o'clock?—you stay behind, without being seen."

◆

"But how can I do that? They'll see me if I don't leave."

"Hide," Mr. Hairston said, impatient suddenly. "There must be a place to hide. You're a small boy. Maybe in the bathroom. Or there must be a back room in the place."

"There's a storeroom," Henry said, and immediately regretted mentioning the storeroom because he was not certain that he wanted to hide anywhere at all at the center.

"Fine. The important thing is to stay behind, out of sight when the others leave."

Henry looked at the window; saw Mr. Selsky in his three-piece blue serge suit sweeping the sidewalk in front of his store across the street.

"You wait awhile. To make sure everyone's gone. Then you come out. . . ."

Henry pictured himself in the evening shadows of the center. It would be spooky, he thought.

"Then you find a hammer. There must be a hammer there, right? You said they have tools of all kinds there. All right, find a hammer. Or even an ax. Something like that . . ."

Has he gone mad? Henry thought.

"What do I do with the hammer?"

"I want you to take the hammer and smash the old man's village. Smash it, break it. . . ."

Henry recoiled as if Mr. Hairston had struck him in the stomach, taking his breath away.

"What's the matter?" Mr. Hairston asked, eyes

◆

like slits, eyebrows touching each other over the bridge of his nose.

Henry could not speak, wincing as he pictured the old man's beloved village smashed and broken by a hammer.

"All right, all right," Mr. Hairston said. "It sounded terrible when I said it like that. But we're not talking about a real village here. It's a fake village."

"I can't do that," Henry managed to utter.

"Sure you can. It's not like you were destroying real property. The village is a toy. The figures the old man made are toy figures. All toys get broken after a while."

"But this is like the old man's own village. Where he grew up. Where his family lived. It means the whole world to him. . . ."

"Listen, it will do him good," Mr. Hairston said. "You told me he was just about finished, didn't you? What will he do now? He'll be unhappy with nothing to do. This way he can rebuild the village, do it all over again, find more pleasure in it. Remember how you said he loses himself in his work? That he's happy when he uses his tools? Well, he'll have a chance to use them again. You see?"

Henry didn't see. But he saw in his mind the destruction of the village and it was a terrible vision, the buildings shattered, the figures broken.

Then jubilantly he saw a way out.

"The village won't be there anymore," he said.

"Mr. Levine won first prize in a contest the city held." Excitement growing in him: "The village is going on display at City Hall."

"When's this happening?" the grocer asked suspiciously, as if Henry was merely making excuses.

"Saturday," he replied. "There's going to be a big ceremony. The mayor will be there."

Surely Mr. Hairston could not deny the old man his moment of glory.

"We have time," the grocer said. "Today is Wednesday. You can do it tomorrow night. Or Friday, at the latest."

"No," Henry cried out, louder than he had intended, the word hanging in the air, echoing in his ears.

Mr. Hairston's eyes flashed at him. For a moment Henry feared that the grocer would actually hit him. Instead he sighed, and when he spoke his voice was calm, almost gentle.

"Don't make a decision now, Henry. Think about it awhile. Think about it tonight. And think about this: If I can't trust you to do this little thing for me, how can I trust you anymore here in the store?" Full of regret. "Don't you see? I will have to let you go. No more paychecks to help at home. No monument for your brother." Tenderly, softly: "Know what else, Henry? I will have to spread the word about you to other merchants. That you are not to be trusted. No one will ever hire you again. Or even let you enter their store." Almost whispering:

"The principal of your school? A friend of mine. I will have to tell him to keep his eye on you. Who knows? Maybe you cheat at school. Someone who can't be trusted often cheats."

Henry listened, dumbfounded, to the grocer's horrible words, made all the more horrible by his tender, gentle voice. He knew without any doubt that Mr. Hairston was capable of doing exactly what he had said he would do.

The grocer cleared his throat. "Well," he said, as if he had just concluded a satisfying piece of business with a customer, "that's the way things stand, Henry. Of course, none of it has to happen. And it would be too bad to do all those things. All I want you to do is break a little toy village. Is that so much to ask for all that I'll do for you?"

Before Henry could speak—and he was not sure that he *could* speak—the grocer held up his hand, like a teacher calling for silence. "No, don't say anything. Think about it, Henry, as I said. Think of all the good things and then the bad things. If you speak now, you might say something you'll regret later. Think it over tonight. At home. In bed. Give me your answer tomorrow."

Henry nodded in agreement, wanting only to get out of this place, away from Mr. Hairston and his suggestions, far far away from his awful plan.

"Don't say anything to anybody," the grocer cautioned as Henry made for the door. "Whether you do this thing for me or not, if you open your mouth to anyone, all those bad things will happen. Maybe worse . . ."

The grocer kept on speaking, but Henry was already out the door.

He lifted the sledgehammer above his head, the huge tool so heavy that it almost threw him backward. Gathering his strength, he slammed the hammer down on the village, smashing two houses and a barn, sending splinters of wood through the air. The sound was enormous, like a bomb falling and exploding. He paused to inspect the damage before lifting the hammer again and saw a figure coming out of the farmhouse. The figure was Mr. Levine, his cap flying from his head, running frantically, looking up in horror as Henry raised the hammer.

A moan of pity and dread came from his mouth as he prepared to smash more of the village, but this time the heavy sledgehammer *did* throw him backward, to the floor, and he woke up in bed, heart racing, the damp sheet clinging to his body, pressed

across his mouth suffocatingly. He leapt from the
dream, found himself sitting up, moonlight like a
white shroud on the floor, his entire body moist. His
fingers trembled as he ran them through his hair.

His mother, who always slept lightly, a part of
her always awake it seemed, called from the next
room. "Is that you, Henry? Is something wrong?"

He realized he must have cried out in his sleep.
"I had a bad dream, Ma."

She appeared at the doorway, ghostlike, a
wraith.

"Want some cocoa?"

"No, I'm all right."

But he was not all right. He dreaded going back
to sleep, afraid that the dream would resume and he
would go on demolishing the village all night long.
While the old man ran from the hammer.

"Ma," he said tentatively, thinking that perhaps
now in the hush of nighttime he could talk to her
about Mr. Hairston's plan.

"What, Henry? What's the matter?"

He did not answer but slipped reluctantly under the sheet. He still could not put into words what
Mr. Hairston had suggested.

"Want to tell me about the dream?" she said,
advancing into the room, her face pale in the moonlight, her dark eyes like two small black caves in her
face. "They say if you tell your dream, it won't come
back again."

How he longed to tell her his dream. And tell

her, too, of his dilemma, the decision he had to make. Instead, he drew the sheet up to his eyes, trying to make himself small in the bed.

"I can barely remember it," he lied, because the sight of the old man scurrying from his house in horror still raced across his mind.

She stroked his head, bent and kissed his forehead. "I'll be awake awhile."

He thought of the empty bed without his father in it awaiting his return. "I'm sorry, Ma," he said. Sorry about so many things he could do nothing about. And now this terrible thing Mr. Hairston wanted him to do.

"Try to think nice thoughts," his mother said, smoothing the sheet as if her hand was treading water.

He tried to think nice thoughts as he huddled in bed, waiting for sleep to come, but could think only of Mr. Hairston and the store. He had often wondered why Mr. Hairston had hired him to work in the store, why he had kept his job open for him when he hurt his leg. Now he knew. When Henry applied for the job, Mr. Hairston had asked, "Can you follow orders? Whether you like them or not?" Henry had answered with a resounding "Yes." "I'll remember that," the grocer had said, his eyes boring into Henry's. He had been looking for someone like Henry and had found him.

Just before he fell off to sleep, Henry thought for the first time: But why? Why did Mr. Hairston want the old man's village destroyed? Weariness plucked at him with gentle fingers, however, and he drifted off gratefully, giving himself over to the merciful blankness of sleep.

Mr. Hairston's calendar on the wall next to the cigarette case was a one-day-at-a-time calendar, showing in big black numbers the date and, in smaller type, the day of the week. Henry's eyes went automatically to the calendar whenever he entered the store, and today was no exception except for the small shock of the number *28* and the bigger shock of *Thursday.*

The grocer looked up as Henry entered, then went back to adding up a customer's order. But as Henry made his way toward the rear of the store, he felt the grocer's eyes following him. Or was this his imagination? How can you feel someone's eyes upon you? Mr. Hairston's eyes were not like anyone else's, however.

Henry fled to the cellar, glad now for his chore of putting up potatoes, listening to the footsteps above, grateful for the customers who kept the grocer busy. Finally, the potatoes were all packed in the bags and Henry reluctantly went back upstairs.

Later, as he rearranged the fruit at the back of the store, he became aware of the silence that meant the absence of customers. He heard Mr. Hairston's footsteps as he left the register and began to walk toward the back of the store. Finally the grocer's shadow fell across the ascending pyramid of oranges.

"Two things," Mr. Hairston said, while Henry continued to work at the fruit.

"Look at me, boy," he ordered.

Henry turned around but avoided the grocer's eyes, concentrating on the buttons of his white coat.

"First, your mother."

The words chilled Henry, caused him to shudder even in the dust and heat of the store.

"She works at the Miss Wickburg Diner," the grocer said, surprise in his voice as if he had just discovered the fact.

"The owner's a friend of mine," the grocer said. "I'm not talking about the manager, who's a softie, who treats help like family. I mean the owner, who doesn't put up with nonsense. . . ."

Henry waited, taking his eyes away from the buttons, afraid he could be hypnotized by concentrating on them.

"A while ago the owner was in trouble, needed money, a loan. He came to me and I helped him out.

That's what people should do, help each other out. Don't you agree, Henry?"

Henry did not reply, looked briefly into the grocer's dark eyes and then went back to the buttons, noticing for the first time one cracked button, second from the top.

"So I helped him out. And he said, 'If there's ever anything I can do for you, just let me know.' Do you see?" Without waiting for a reply he continued. "So, with your mother, if I tell the owner to give her a raise, give her better hours, make her a hostess, even, so she doesn't have to wait on tables anymore, he'll do it." He snapped his fingers. "Like that."

Henry braced himself, knew what was coming, had known what was coming all the time, of course.

"On the other hand, if things don't go right, then a word to the owner can have the opposite effect. If I say, 'Fire this woman or that woman,' then he'll do it. Of course, I would not want to do that. The owner says your mother is a very nice woman. A good waitress. She deserves a raise. And a promotion. Why not—right, Henry? You love your mother, don't you? It's in your hands. . . ." The grocer sighed.

"Such a small thing I'm asking you to do. Look at all the rewards for doing it."

If it's such a small thing, why is it so important to you? Henry asked, but silently. Afraid of the answer, afraid of what the grocer might say.

"Now, the second thing," the grocer said, glancing anxiously at the door—but no one entered.

"If you are going to do this thing, then do it today, tonight. You said the display will be moved Saturday morning, but they might change their minds and do it tomorrow. You can never tell about people. So, I don't want you to wait." He looked at his watch. "It's now almost three. You can leave in a few minutes."

Henry remained silent, listening to his heartbeat. "Whether you do it or not, I want you to leave now, this minute. If you do this thing, then come back after. I'll be waiting here in the store, you'll see the light on. If you don't, then never come back." He reached into his coat pocket, took out some folded dollar bills. "Here's your pay for the week." He tucked the money into Henry's shirt pocket. "I never want to see you again if you fail to do what I ask."

The customer bell finally rang and Henry, gratefully, saw Mrs. Karminski entering, her small dog sniffing and yipping as usual.

A few minutes later, as Henry headed toward the door, the grocer called his name. Henry paused, his hand on the doorknob. He heard the grocer's approaching footsteps.

"Do it," the grocer whispered in his ear. "Destroy the old man's village."

Henry turned, stepped aside, curious to see the expression on the grocer's face after issuing such a terrible order. He was surprised to see, not something ugly or repulsive, but the bland everyday face of Mr. Hairston. But he shuddered, opening the door, as if he had just touched the glistening skin of a snake.

--- ❖ ❖ ❖ ---

I'm going to the craft center but I won't smash the village. I will go there and watch the old man at work and talk to George Graham but I won't do what Mr. Hairston wants me to do.

Glad to be free of the grocer and the store, Henry raced through the twisted streets, waiting for the pain that always came when he ran too fast or too far. Pushing himself to the limit, he invited the pain, breathless, sweating, the sweat blurring his vision. Finally he paused near a telephone pole, gasping, his breath sounding like a piece of cloth being torn in two.

Leaning against the pole, oblivious to anyone who might be watching, he heard the grocer's voice: "Such a little thing I'm asking you to do, and think of all the rewards." The monument for Eddie, his mother's raise and promotion, his own job saved. The old man's village only a toy village, really.

When he arrived at the center, he paused again to catch his breath. Looking down the street, he saw the same wise guys in front of the saloon, not gambling with coins now but merely lounging about lazily. Henry envied them for doing nothing, no orders to follow, no terrible deeds to carry out.

The center bustled with activity and excitement; somebody sweeping, somebody else washing the walls, while others worked at their benches as usual.

The old man was not in sight but George Graham greeted him, turning away from the woman with blue hair who was molding another child's face from clay. She plucked delicately at the eyes.

The old man's village was not covered with the sheet. The figures and the buildings glowed brilliantly beneath the shaded light. "Mr. Levine polished everything with a secret mixture," the giant said. "He didn't come today, resting up, waiting for his big day." He gestured with his hand. "We're sprucing up the place. Big doings, Henry, big doings . . ."

He rushed off in answer to a workman calling for assistance and Henry began to search the place with his eyes. Searching for what? A hammer, just in case. He was convinced that he would not find a hammer suitable for the job, and thus would have no chance to do what Mr. Hairston wanted him to do. He avoided looking at the old man's village.

Everyone was too busy to pay any attention to him and he wandered through the center unnoticed, invisible. He spotted a wooden mallet leaning against the wall near the door to the storeroom. Like a croquet mallet but bigger and heavier, as big as a sledgehammer but made of wood. Henry glanced away, not wanting to acknowledge its presence.

"Watch out," a workman called, carrying a ladder with which to reach a burned-out bulb on the ceiling.

Henry ducked out of the way and found himself in front of the storeroom door. The storeroom was a place he seldom entered, windowless, cluttered with the paraphernalia of the center. Glancing around, he was glad to see that he was still being ignored. He opened the door and slipped inside. He turned on the light, saw a haphazard collection of old boxes, discarded tools, paint cans, rubbish barrels.

A perfect place to hide.

The mallet out there and this place to hide in. He wondered if he was destined to carry out his mission after all. Was it such a bad mission? A few smashed figures that the old man could make again balanced against all the good things that might happen. His mother a hostess instead of a waitress . . .

He snapped off the light and stood still, his eyes becoming accustomed to the darkness. When he

◆

could make out shapes and forms, he walked slowly, gingerly, to a spot where cardboard boxes were piled up. Kicked something, and heard it thud against the wall. Paused, not moving, then slipped into a corner. He piled some boxes on top of one another, then crept behind them and sat down, certain that he could not be seen if someone entered.

He calculated that he had two hours to wait.

Through the closed door he could hear the sounds of activity in the center, muffled voices, footsteps, chairs scraping the floor.

Drawing up his knees, he embraced them with his arms, rested his forehead on them. Pictured his mother in a white lace apron leading customers to their tables, handing them menus, earning a salary, no longer depending on tips. And pictured, too, the monument on Eddie's grave, the ball and bat signifying his prowess at the plate so that anyone visiting the cemetery would be reminded of how great a ballplayer he had been.

He did not realize he had fallen asleep until he awoke, like being shot out of a cannon. Into nothingness, blankness, grayness, and then the workroom, the boxes piled in front of him. Blinking, he listened. Something had awakened him—what? Listened again, tilting his head. Then heard it: a soft scratching nearby, then the rustle of small feet, scurrying. He shivered, realizing there was a rat in the storeroom. He remembered now the stories George Graham had told of rats coming out at night, gnawing at the brushes and the canvases. *I've got to get out of here.*

Walking blindly, stumbling once, he made his way to the door. He opened it cautiously, peered out, saw the deserted center, a small bulb dimly glowing near the front door. Sheets covered easels and benches, turning them into ghosts of all shapes and sizes. His gaze fell on the mallet.

Such a little thing to do, the grocer had said.

He picked up the mallet and walked on legs still stiff from the cramped position of his sleep to the old man's bench. The mallet was heavy and he put it down. He removed the sheet, careful not to disturb the figures. Letting the sheet fall gently to the floor, he gazed upon the village in the dim light of the distant bulb. The village and its inhabitants were caught in a kind of twilight. He touched the figure of the man as a boy, the blue cap on his head, the dark jacket. A toy, really. All the figures toys. Not a real village and not real people.

Don't think. Do it.

He picked up the mallet. Raised it above his head. The weight of the mallet sent him slightly off balance and he swayed a bit. Sweat broke out on his forehead like small explosions from his pores. His hair was suddenly damp, a moist lock falling across his forehead. Fastening his grip on the mallet as he held it aloft, he looked down at the village.

Such a simple thing. You don't have to do any-

thing. Let the mallet do it. Let it drop, like an atomic bomb falling from a plane.

Blood drained from his arms above his head into his shoulders, flooding his heart, causing it to thump dangerously in his chest.

Do it.

But could not.

Could not move either.

He stood frozen like a statue in a park or a church, utterly unable to move, the pain spreading throughout his body now, his heartbeats thudding in his temples. Trapped this way, as if for eternity.

Then, a small darting movement to his left at the corner of his vision. Looking down, unable to move anything except his eyes, he saw a rat leaping to the bench, saw it slithering among the buildings and figures. Henry, too, leapt, startled, gasping, dropping the mallet, then watching in horror as it smashed into the village, splintering the farmhouse, sending figures askew, the old man's mother spilling out of the window. Other figures, including the old man as a boy, tumbling and falling and then the bench itself breaking in two, like a crack in the surface caused by an earthquake, the building and figures disappearing into the crack.

A sound came from deep inside him . . . *Ahhhhhh* . . . like the sound the old man had made the day Henry told him about Eddie's death, a sound of anguish and heartache that filled the center as Henry looked down at the ruined village. The village blurred as his eyes filled with tears.

The silence in the center was almost deafening.

Get out of here.

Get far away.

He swiveled away from the broken bench, unable any longer to gaze at the horror of his accomplishment. He stalked toward the door on legs as stiff as wooden stilts. *I didn't want to do it.*

But he had done it, after all.

❖ ❖ ❖

A thundering waterfall greeted him as he stepped out into the dismal and deserted street, lit up suddenly by a flash of lightning. He drew back, pressing himself against the door.

He knew that he could not risk hanging around the center. Someone might spot him here and remember his presence later. Despite another flash of lightning and the instant boom of thunder that followed, he dashed onto the sidewalk, hunching his shoulders against the rain and a sudden blast of wind. His breath caught as he raced along. Rounding a corner gasping, he came face to face with Mr. Hairston.

"In here," Mr. Hairston said, indicating the doorway of a furniture store closed for the night. Thunder boomed again and Henry ducked in beside the grocer. His wet clothes clung to his body.

He had never seen the grocer outside of the store before. He was smaller, thinner, shivering with the chill of the rain.

"I've been waiting for you," he said, eyes bright with anticipation. "Did you do it? Is the village smashed?"

"The village is smashed," Henry said, his voice cracking as he spoke.

Rain beat against the store windows.

"Excellent, excellent," Mr. Hairston said, briskly rubbing his hands together, savoring his moment. He reached out as if to embrace Henry and Henry pulled away.

"I smashed the village," he said, "but it was an accident. I didn't mean to do it."

"How could it be an accident?" the grocer asked.

"I found a big mallet and was ready to use it. But couldn't." He saw doubt leaping in the grocer's eyes and raised his voice. "I didn't want to do it." Then sighed. "A rat jumped on the bench. I dropped the mallet. It smashed the village."

"How bad?" the grocer asked, warily.

"Bad enough," Henry said. "Bad enough so that it won't go to City Hall. Bad enough to ruin it."

"Congratulations," the grocer said. "You did it, then. Whether you wanted to or not, you did it." Astonishingly, he winked at Henry, the wink drawing them into a kind of conspiracy, and Henry backed away against the cold glass of the window.

"I'm a man of my word, Henry. You'll keep your job and have a raise. I'll speak to the owner about your mother's promotion. And the monument—I'll order it first chance I get. . . ."

For the first time the enormity of Mr. Hairston's offer stunned Henry. Why all these rewards for wrecking what the grocer regarded as a toy village?

"Why?" he asked, the word almost lost in a boom of thunder.

"Why what?" Frowning, surprised, the grocer looked sharply at him.

"Why do all those things for me? Why was it so important to smash the old man's village? Why do you hate him so much?"

"He's a Jew," the grocer said. As if that explained it all.

Truly puzzled, Henry said, "You could have hired some wise guys to do it. Pay them a few dollars. Why me?"

"You're a good boy, Henry. You're honest, you work hard. You're good to your mother. You worry about your father. You want to buy a monument for your brother. You feel bad for an old Jew. Such a good boy." There was mockery in his voice. "I'll bet you say your prayers every night. So good, so innocent . . ."

"But smashing the village was a bad thing," Henry said, with dawning recognition of a truth too incredible to understand. "You wanted me to do a bad thing."

The grocer smiled, not his inside-out-sneer behind his customers' backs but a ghastly smile, like
the smile on a Halloween mask.

Astonished, Henry thought:

*It was me he was after all the time. Not just the
old man and his village. He didn't want me to be
good anymore.*

The grocer regarded him with affection, as if
Henry were a favorite son. "You see, Henry, you are
like the rest of us, after all. Not so innocent, are you?
Yes, the rat surprised you. But you went to the center and found the mallet. Raised it above your head.
Smashed the village. None of that would have happened if you hadn't wanted the rewards."

Henry shriveled against the window, needing to
move farther away from the grocer but trapped in
the doorway.

"I don't want your rewards," he said.

The grocer waved away his protest. "Of course
you do. You earned them. The village is wrecked.
You won't restore it by refusing."

"No," Henry said. "I'm quitting the job. I don't
want it. Eddie wouldn't want your monument either. And my mother, leave her alone. . . ."

"But you have to accept these things," the grocer said. "We made a bargain."

"Keep your bargain," Henry said.

"No, *you* must keep it," the grocer insisted.
"When you smashed the village, you kept one part
of it. Now you have to do the rest. Come on, Henry."

A new note in the grocer's voice, one that Henry barely recognized. "It's not complete unless you accept the rewards."

Henry shook his head. "No," he shouted against the drumming rain.

"Please," the grocer said.

Please?

He saw suddenly that the rewards were just as important to the grocer as smashing the village.

"No," he said again, with deadly determination.

"You must accept. You must let me do this. It's very important. Otherwise, the smashing means nothing. . . ." Pleading in his voice.

Taking a deep breath, Henry ran out of the doorway, brushing by the grocer, sending him spinning, out into a torrent of rain, instantly soaked, shivering, bumping against a mailbox, almost falling. Regaining his balance, he looked back to see the grocer standing in the rain, wet and dripping, a pathetic figure calling, "Please, Henry, come back, you must come back."

Henry shook his head, whirled, ran again, ignoring the rain and his soaked clothing, ran until, out of breath, he paused at the entrance of an abandoned theater. Shrank into the shadows, shivering, not from the rain but because he knew at last what Mr. Hairston was.

He huddled miserably in the doorway, waiting for the rain to stop.

They moved back to Frenchtown three weeks later, the day after his father was discharged from the hospital. "It was a mistake coming here," his mother said. "You can't run away from the past. We tried to forget Eddie and that was wrong."

His father was not cured, of course, and still sat quietly for hours at a time. But he smiled sometimes and actually helped pack up their belongings for the trip home. "It'll be good to go back," he said as he closed a suitcase. Henry and his mother exchanged smiles of gratitude.

In the days following the destruction of the old man's village, Henry avoided walking by the grocery store and did not approach the craft center. He also was careful to avoid encountering the old man at eight in the morning and late in the afternoon.

He looked in the newspaper for a story, either about the exhibition at City Hall or the smashing of the village, but did not see one.

He did not have nightmares but awoke sometimes to a strange sound in his bedroom and realized that the sound was himself crying.

He began hanging around the yard behind the store, hoping to catch a glimpse of Doris. Occasionally, a woman appeared on the second-floor piazza and hung clothes on a reel or banged a mop on the banister, sending a blizzard of dust down below.

Finally, he saw Doris coming down the stairs, moving tentatively as usual, library books cradled in her arms.

He waited until she was into the alley, then stepped in front of her.

Startled to see him, she drew away. "Are you all right?" she asked, whispering even away from the store.

"I quit my job," he said.

"He said he fired you."

Henry shook his head. "Don't believe him. I know he's your father but he's . . ."

"What?" she asked. "What is he?" Curiosity curling her words, she leaned forward, as if she was about to learn for the first time who her father was.

Henry avoided the word he wanted to use. How could he tell the girl that her father was an evil man? "Your father's weak, Doris," he said. "And he's afraid. You have to stand up to him. Don't let him call you clumsy and hurt you anymore.''

She stepped back, looking fearfully over his shoulder, and he knew she was looking to see if her father had followed her.

"He got me to do a bad thing, Doris," he said. "I didn't want to do it but I did it. Then he wanted to give me rewards for doing it. But I didn't take them.''

He could see that his words meant nothing to her and he knew he could never explain to her, or to anyone, even a priest in confession, what had really happened that night.

"The important thing is that I stood up to him," he said. "And there was nothing he could do about it. Nothing. Stand up to him, Doris.''

"He's my father," she said, with simple terrible truth.

He knew then what he had to do. Even though he was moving away, he had to help her. Had to come back, whenever he could, no matter the distance, to see her. He didn't know how he could do this but knew he was pledged to do so.

"I've got to go," she said. "He expects me back to help in the store. He gets mad if I'm gone too long.''

"We're moving, Doris. Back to Frenchtown," he said.

A flash of something in her eyes. Sorrow, regret? He could not tell.

♦

"I'll come back and visit," he said. "Maybe we can meet at the library."

She looked at him for a long moment, seemed about to speak, then reached out and touched his cheek with fingers that trembled on his flesh. "Thank you," she whispered. She hurried away, almost running.

"I *will* come back," he called out to her as she disappeared around the corner.

Loneliness, almost unbearable, seized him.

He gathered his courage finally and went to the craft center to say good-bye. Took a deep breath and opened the door. George Graham greeted him with a cheerful shout. "It's good to see you, Henry. Where have you been?"

Henry glanced quickly toward Mr. Levine's bench and was glad to see the old man busy at work, hands moving delicately as usual, the bench restored. The village lay spread out before him, sparser than before, not so many buildings or figures. The old man looked up and smiled radiantly at him.

"Did you hear what happened?" the giant asked. Mercifully, he went on before Henry could answer. "Some wise guys, probably from down the street, invaded the place. Damaged Mr. Levine's village but must have been scared off. They didn't finish the job, didn't have time to touch any other benches. . . ."

"Poor Mr. Levine," Henry said, wondering if the guilt in his eyes was visible.

"Look at him," the giant said. "A survivor. He just started over again. Nothing can defeat him. The exhibition has been postponed. Maybe till Christmastime." Scrutinizing Henry from his great height, he said, "We missed you, Henry. Is everything all right with you? Your family?"

"We're moving back to Frenchtown," he said.

The giant relayed the news to Mr. Levine, who got to his feet and embraced Henry. They held each other for a long moment.

"Wait," the old man said, reaching into his black bag. He drew out a small figure and placed it in Henry's hand. Henry recognized himself, his blue shirt, the tousled hair that never stayed combed. He studied the big smile on the tiny wooden face. Henry Cassavant, three inches high, but smiling and sturdy. He would keep this figure for the rest of his life and look at it sometimes and remember this summer. Someday, perhaps, he would be able to look at it and return the smile.

In the evening of the first day back in Frenchtown, he searched the drawers and closets of the tenement until he found what he was looking for. He ducked out of the house and made his way to St. Jude's Cemetery. Dusk was gathering, a spooky fog. He speared Eddie's old bat into the soft earth of the grave. He put the scarred and lopsided baseball at the base of the bat. He stepped back, admiring the effect. He did not know how long they would remain before being snatched away, but for this one moment, this one evening, Eddie had his monument.

He knelt and began to pray. Prayed for his father and mother and Eddie's soul in case he was still in purgatory. Prayed for Doris and the old man. And the giant. When he whispered "Deliver us from evil" at the end of the Our Father, he thought of Mr. Hairston. Then he did something he had never done before. He prayed for Mr. Hairston. "Forgive him," he whispered.

Forgive me too.

He continued to kneel there as dusk deepened into night, bringing a chill that raced along his bare arms, and the bat and ball caught the first light of an emerging moon.

ABOUT THE AUTHOR

Robert Cormier is a former journalist and the author of several brilliant and controversial novels for young adults. His books have been translated into many languages and have consistently appeared on the Best Books of the Year for Young Adults lists of the American Library Association, *The New York Times,* and *School Library Journal.* His most recent novel for Delacorte Press was *We All Fall Down.* He is also the winner of the 1991 Margaret A. Edwards Award for a body of work.

Robert Cormier was born in Leominster, Massachusetts, and attended Fitchburg State College. In 1977 the college awarded him an honorary Doctor of Letters degree. He and his wife, Connie, live in Leominster. They have four grown children.